I Can Share!
by Karen Katz

Grosset & Dunlap
An Imprint of Penguin Group (USA) Inc.

Copyright © 2004 by Karen Katz. All rights reserved. This edition published in 2011 by Grosset & Dunlap, a division of Penguin Young Readers Group, 345 Hudson Street, New York, New York 10014. GROSSET & DUNLAP is a trademark of Penguin Group (USA) Inc. Manufactured in China.

ISBN 978-0-448-45592-1   10 9 8 7 6 5 4 3 2 1
Special Markets ISBN 978-0-448-45774-1

MY NEW DOLL!

You can't have her.

But maybe . . .

you can play with this doll.

MY BIKE!

You can't ride it.

But maybe . . .

I'll take you for a ride.

MY SHOVEL! You can't dig with it. But maybe . . .

we can make
a castle
together!

MY SNACK!

You can't eat it.

But maybe . . .

I'll give you
a box of
your own.

MY FRIEND!
You can't play with her. But maybe . . .

we can all play dress-up!

Now I know how to share . . .

and I like it!